CITY STORM

by Mary Jessie Parker

Illustrated by Lynne Dennis

Scholastic Inc. / *New York*

Library of Congress Cataloging-in-Publication Data available.
Library of Congress Number 89-6251
ISBN 0-590-42307-X
12 11 10 9 8 7 6 5 4 3 2 1   0 1 2 3 4/9
Printed in the U.S.A.   36
First Scholastic printing, October 1990
Designed by Anna DiVito

For Adela and Jennifer, with empathy
—M.J.P.

For Jean Maurice
—L.D.

Sun shines.

Vendors call.
People rush.
Children tug.

Clouds form.
Skies darken.

Rumblings sound.

Winds lash.
Hats sail.
Litter swirls.

Children cling.
Parents comfort.

Raindrops splash.
Vendors pack.

Umbrellas open.
Windows close.

Clouds race.
Lightning flashes.
Thunder crashes.

People scurry.

Rain pours.
People huddle.

They wait.

Lightning flares.
Thunder roars.
Dogs hide.

Birds tremble.

Leaves float.
Drains clog.

Tires splash.
Wipers slap.

Headlights shine.

Thunder rumbles.
Showers slow.

Sun peeks.
Skies clear.

Windows open.
Umbrellas close.

Dogs shake.
Birds bathe.

Vendors call.
People rush.
Children tug.

Rainbow glows.